KNOCK! KNOCK!

by Jan Wahl

illustrated by
Mary Newell DePalma

Henry Holt and Company
New York

To Janice and Zachary Dempster, with hugs
—J. W.

Henry Holt and Company, LLC
Publishers since 1866
115 West 18th Street
New York, New York 10011
www.henryholt.com

Henry Holt is a registered trademark of Henry Holt and Company, LLC
Text copyright © 2004 by Jan Wahl
Illustrations copyright © 2004 by Mary Newell DePalma
All rights reserved.
Distributed in Canada by H. B. Fenn and Company Ltd.

Library of Congress Cataloging-in-Publication Data
Wahl, Jan.
Knock! knock! / by Jan Wahl; illustrated by Mary Newell DePalma.
Summary: A little witch sitting alone at her spinning wheel hears a knock at her door,
but the various body parts that enter are not much company.
[1. Witches–Fiction. 2. Body, Human–Fiction.] I. DePalma, Mary Newell, ill. II. Title.
PZ7.W1266Kn 2004   [E]–dc22   2003020997

ISBN 0-8050-6280-7 / EAN 978-0-8050-6280-9
First Edition–2004 / Designed by Amy Manzo Toth
Printed in the United States of America on acid-free paper. ∞

10 9 8 7 6 5 4 3 2 1

The artist used acrylic paint and mixed media to create the illustrations for this book.

This happened a long time ago in Scotland. . . .

Witch Ella La Grimble sat spinning at her spinning wheel. The sun sank down, shining copper bright in a purple-pink sky. She sat alone. How she wished for company!

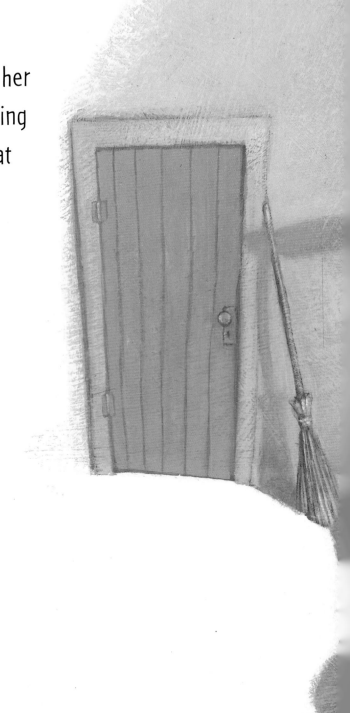

Knock! Knock! at the door. In walked a pair of great big feet and stood before the fire.

"Oh my," said Witch Ella. But feet are not much company.

Knock! Knock! at the door. In marched
a pair of teeny-weeny legs and sat right down
on the great big feet.

An owl hooted outside. Witch Ella sat and
she spun. But legs are not much company.

Knock! Knock! at the door. In hopped a pair of tough
hard knees and sat right down on the teeny-weeny legs.
     The cat hid in the cupboard. Witch Ella sat and she spun.
But knees are not much company.

Knock! Knock! at the door. In leaped a pair of huge fat hips and sat right down on the hard tough knees.

A cricket sang his song. Witch Ella sat and she spun. But hips are not much company.

Knock! Knock! at the door. In waltzed an itty-bitty waist and sat right down on the huge fat hips.

A mouse scratched in the wall. Witch Ella sat and she spun. But a waist is not much company.

the latitude of the British Isles i.e. they

Knock! Knock! at the door. In bounced a pair of broad hairy shoulders and sat right down on the itty-bitty waist.

A slate banged on the roof. Witch Ella sat and she spun. But shoulders are not much company.

Knock! Knock! at the door. In slithered a pair of long bent arms and sat right down on the broad hairy shoulders.

Soup boiled on the hearth. Witch Ella sat and she spun. But arms are not much company.

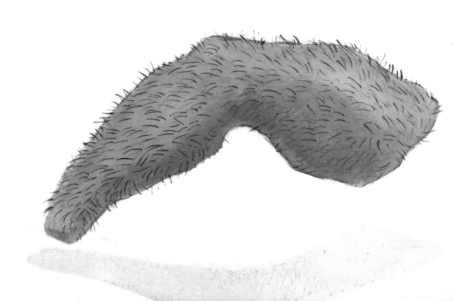

Knock! Knock! at the door. In skipped a pair of thick round hands and sat right down on the long bent arms.

A dog bayed at the top of Dark Hill. Witch Ella sat and she spun. But hands are not much company.

Knock! Knock! at the door. In crawled a wee small neck and sat right down on the broad hairy shoulders.

At last the night grew silent. The moon blinked. Witch Ella sat and she spun. But a neck is not much company.

Knock! Knock! at the door. In rolled
a pumpkin-sized head and sat right down on
the wee small neck.

anything th

kind, size, and

"Oh my!" said Witch Ella La Grimble—a little bit nervous.
Then she asked quietly, "Why do you have such great big feet?"
  "From lots of walking. Lots of walking."

  "Why do you have such teeny-weeny legs?"
  "To hold up my tough hard knees."

  "Why do you have such tough hard knees?"
  "From lots of kneeling. Lots of kneeling."

"Why do you have such an itty-bitty waist?"
"To hold up my broad hairy shoulders."

"Why do you have such broad hairy shoulders?"
"From carrying broom. Carrying broom."

"Why do you have such long bent arms?"
"To hold my hands. To hold my hands."

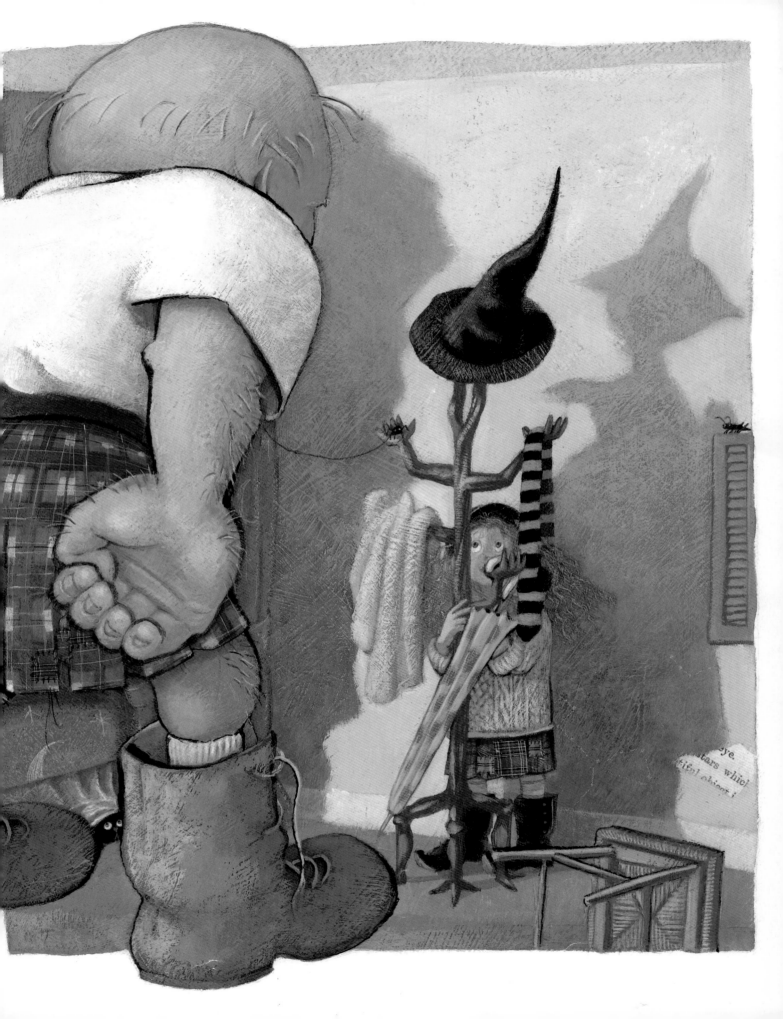

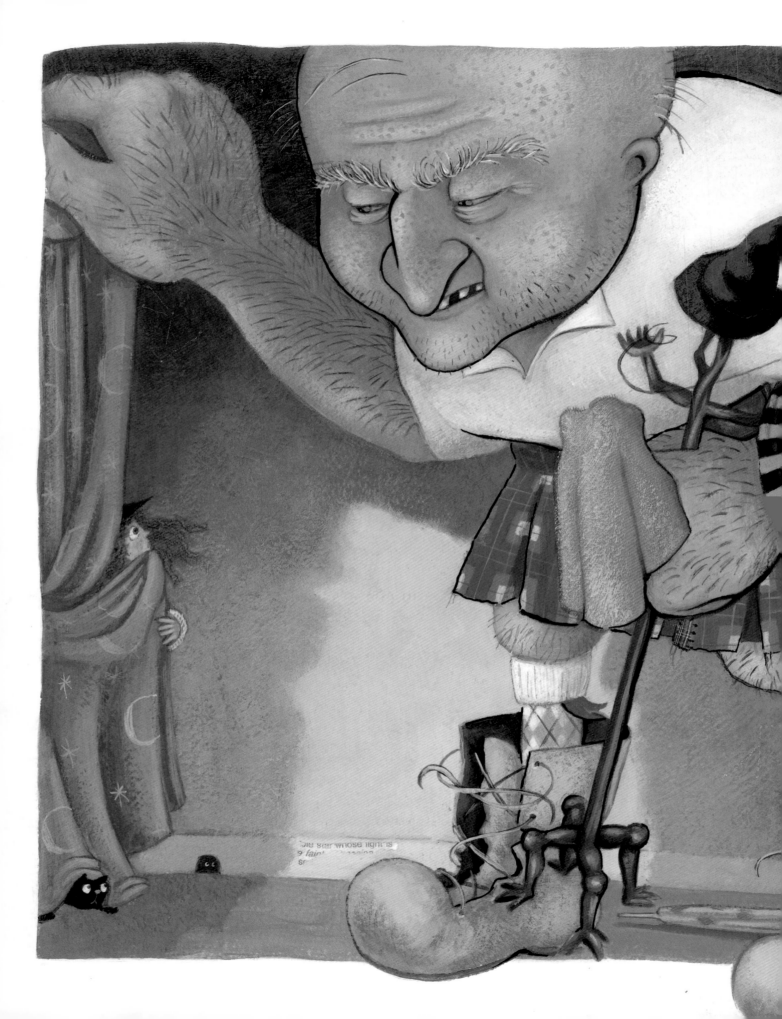

"Why do you have such thick round hands?"
"From raking the fields. Raking the fields."

"Why do you have such a wee small neck?"
"To hold up my head. To hold up my head."

"Why do you have such a pumpkin-sized
head?" she asked.
"Big brain, witch! Big brain."

He came closer.

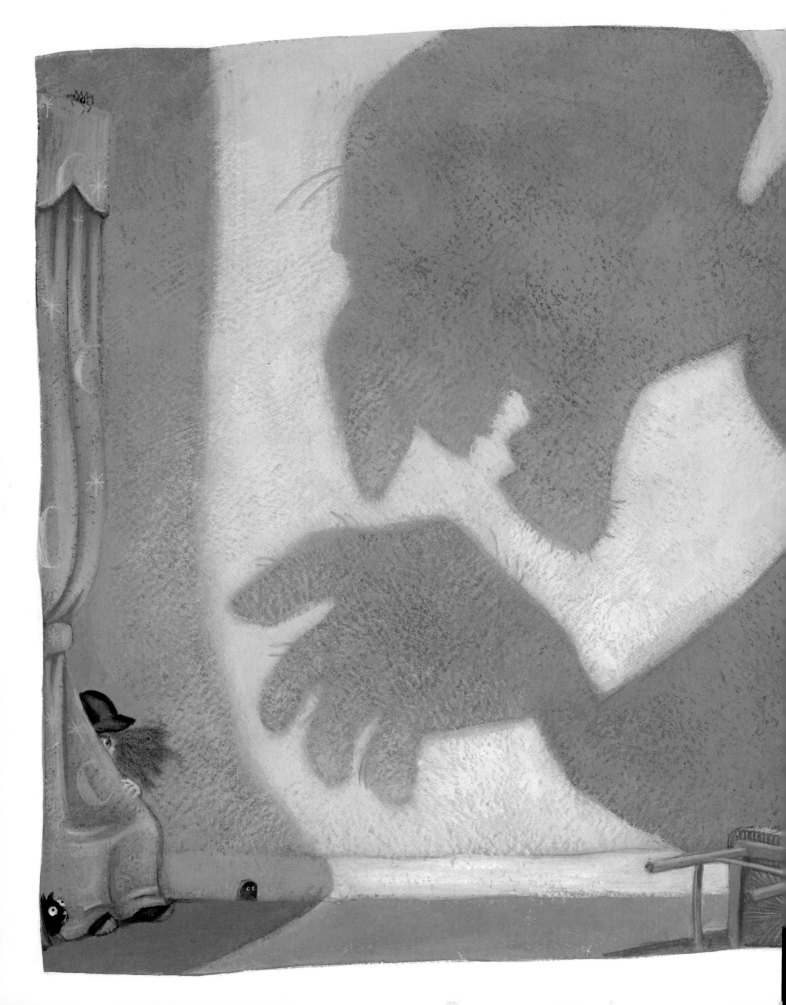

Witch Ella La Grimble asked in a very tiny voice,
"And what do all of you come here for?"

"For YOU, witch, for you . . .

. . . to keep you company!"